ESCAPE FROM PLANET ALCATRAZ

THE PIT OF NO RETURN

BY MICHAEL DAHL

ILLUSTRATED BY PATRICIO CLAREY

Raintree is an imprint of Capstone Global Library Limited, a company
incorporated in England and Wales having its registered office at 264
Banbury Road, Oxford, OX2 7DY – Registered company number: 6695582

www.raintree.co.uk
myorders@raintree.co.uk

Edited by Aaron J Sautter
Designed by Kay Fraser
Original illustrations © Capstone Global Library Limited 2020
Production by Katy LaVigne
Originated by Capstone Global Library Ltd
Printed and bound in India

ISBN: 978 1 4747 8489 4 (paperback)

British Library Cataloguing in Publication Data
A full catalogue record for this book is available from the British Library.

Acknowledgements
Design elements: Shutterstock: Agustina Camilion, A-Star, Dima Zel,
Draw_Wing_Zen, Hybrid_Graphics, Metallic Citizen

CONTENTS

ERRO

PLATEAU of LENG

PHANTOM FOREST

POISON SEA

VULCAN MOUNTAINS

LAKE of GOLD

METAL MOON

DIAMOND MINES

MONSTER ZOO

PITS OF NO RETURN

PRISON STRONGHOLDS

SWAMP OF FLAME

SCARLET JUNGLE

PRISON ENERGY DRIVES

SPACE PORT PRISONER INTAKE

ABYSS OF GIANTS

ZAK

THE PRISONERS

ZAK NINE

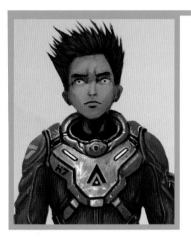

Zak is a teenage boy from Earth Base Zeta. He dreams of piloting a star fighter one day. Zak is very brave and is a quick thinker. But his enthusiasm often leads him into trouble.

ERRO

Erro is a teenage furling from the planet Quom. He has the fur, long tail, sharp eyes and claws of his species. Erro is often impatient with Zak's reckless ways. But he shares his friend's love of adventure.

THE PRISON PLANET

Alcatraz . . . there is no escape from this terrifying prison planet. It's filled with dungeons, traps, endless deserts, and other dangers. Zak Nine and his alien friend, Erro, are trapped here. They had sneaked onto a ship hoping to see an awesome space battle. But the ship landed on Alcatraz instead. Now they have to work together if they ever hope to escape!

ERRO'S STORY . . . CAUGHT! >>>

My friend Zak and I tried to run. But nobody can escape the Shadow Guard for long. The guards caught us and are taking us to a new part of Alcatraz. All we can do is follow their orders as they march us across this endless, empty plain. . . .

>>>>

CHAPTER ONE:
CAPTURED

Four guards are forcing us to walk ahead of them. They wear thick, black armour with spiked helmets.

They also carry laser spears. I do not like sharp objects. One guard pushes my friend along.

"Hey, watch who you're shoving there, pal!" says Zak.

Zak is never afraid to say what he thinks.

Zak and I have been captured. Again. Will we ever get off this prison planet?

"You won't escape this time," the guards' leader growls at us. The others laugh cruelly.

They prod us across a huge metal platform with their laser spears. Suddenly, the platform rumbles, and the air is full of steam.

"What is that hole?" I whisper. My tail is twitching nervously.

Zak shakes his head. "I can't see a hole."

I forgot. Human eyes are weak. They cannot see through steam like we Quomlings can.

The steam rolls aside. We see a dark, round pit in the metal floor. The guards force us to the very edge.

"Welcome to your new home!" shouts one of the guards.

The guards shove their laser spears at us. They push us over the edge and into the dark hole!

CHAPTER TWO:
THE SINKING PIT

We tumble into the pit and land on a smooth metal floor.

The guards stare down at us. "Welcome to the Pit of No Return," says the leader with a snort.

I look up to study the hole. Clouds of steam roll by the pit's opening high above us.

I feel the smooth walls with my paws.

"This is too easy," says Zak, rubbing his shoulder. "I bet we can climb out of here, no problem."

Meanwhile, I examine the wall.

"What are you looking at?" Zak asks, walking towards me.

WHOOOOOSHHHH! BANG!

I am almost knocked off my feet.
The pit is suddenly deeper.

"This is crazy!" says Zak. He steps
towards the middle of the pit.

WHOOOOOSHHHH! BANG!

The floor sinks again. The top of
the pit is now even further away.

CHAPTER THREE:
SINKING LAYER BY LAYER

"Do not move!" I warn Zak, sticking out my paw.

"Each time we do, the floor sinks deeper," I explain.

Zak squints at the wall.

"This pit must be like a spyglass," he says. "I think the wall has metal layers that fit inside each other."

"See, it probably extends . . ."
He steps up next to me, pointing
towards the wall.

WHOOOOOSHHHH! BANG!

"You did it again!" I say.

"I forgot!" he shouts.

The guards' snorts and laughter
echo above us.

HA-HA-HA-HA-HA-HA!

CHAPTER FOUR:
CLIMBING CRACK BY CRACK

I clap my paws over both ears.

"Please, do not shout," I say.
"My hearing is very sensitive."

"Sorry," says Zak.

We stand still for a full hour.
The guards grow bored and leave.

"I've got an idea," Zak says suddenly. "Use your claws to climb up."

"I cannot climb up smooth metal!"

"Try using the cracks between the different layers," he says.

I look down at my claws. I admit they are excellent at gripping things.

"I'll give you a boost," says Zak.

Zak laces his fingers together and looks at me with a smirk. "Hop on."

I think he wants me to step on his soft, clawless hands. I carefully do as he asks.

His hands are warmer than I expected. "How do you humans stay warm without fur?" I ask.

"Just comes naturally," he says with a shrug. "Ready?"

I nod, and Zak suddenly flips me high into the air.

I slam into the wall. Hard.

"You did it!" says Zak, jumping up and down. "You caught the crack!"

I look up at my claws. Zak is right! I am gripping the thin crack between the panels.

CHAPTER FIVE: PRESSURE

"You can do it," says Zak. "Climb up and find a rope or something for me to climb."

I slowly climb the smooth metal.

My strong claws and keen eyes quickly find more cracks. Soon I am moving faster and faster.

"Use your tail to balance," Zak calls out.

"I know how to climb!" I say. "Do not be so bossy."

When I reach the top, I cautiously pop my head out.

I stare through the steam clouds. No guards are around.

I see something that looks like rope. I scurry over to fetch it.

But it is not a rope. It is a thick rubber hose.

An air hose! I think. *The pit's floor must move using air pressure.*

I look around and see an air valve nearby. I pull the air hose behind me and screw it into the valve.

I can't hear any air. Maybe if I push this little red button . . .

WHOOOOOOOOOOOOOSH!

The floor rumbles.

"Aaaaaaaaahhh!" I hear Zak scream.

What have I done?!

Then I hear heavy footsteps and see a guard standing over me.

The guard snarls and aims his laser spear at me. "*Nobody* returns from the Pit!" he growls.

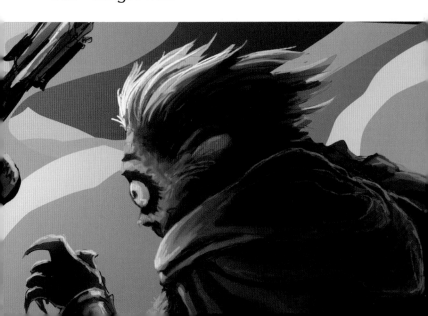

But then I see a dark object fall from above.

THUD!

Zak has fallen through the steam and landed on the guard. The guard is on the floor, knocked out.

"The floor of the pit was moving up fast!" says Zak. "It threw me in the air like a catapult!"

The guard is beginning to groan.

"We'd better get out of here," Zak says. He gets up and brushes the dust off his clothes.

The Pit and the guard soon disappear as we run into the clouds of steam. Hopefully, this will be our final escape. . . .

GLOSSARY

cruelly knowingly do something in a way that causes pain or discomfort

dungeon prison, usually underground

keen having the ability to see or notice things easily

laser thin, intense beam of light

layer single thickness of something

panel flat piece of material made to form part of a surface

prod poke or jab at with a pointed object

scurry hurry or run with short, quick steps

species group of living things that share similar features

spyglass small telescope with several sections that fit inside one another

valve moveable part that controls the flow of liquid or gas through a pipe

TALK ABOUT IT

1. Erro sees the Pit through the steam before Zak can. Why do you think he can see it first? What makes Erro's alien eyes able to see better than human eyes?

2. Every time the boys move at the bottom of the Pit, its floor sinks deeper. What do you think causes this? Can you think of anything in real life that reacts to your movements?

3. The air near the Pit is filled with a lot of steam. Where do you think the steam is coming from? Why is there so much of it? Discuss how the steam might be used to power the Pit.

WRITE ABOUT IT

1. Zak and Erro have to work together to get out of the Pit. Write about a time when you had to work with someone else to accomplish a task. Explain why two people had to work together to achieve success.

2. Imagine you are a young Quom furling like Erro. Write a short story about growing up on Quom. Explain what life is like there and how useful large eyes, strong claws and a flexible tail are on Erro's home planet.

ABOUT THE AUTHOR

Michael Dahl is the author of more than 300 books for young readers, including the Library of Doom series. He is a huge fan of Star Trek, Star Wars and Doctor Who. He has a fear of closed-in spaces, but has visited several prisons, dungeons and strongholds, both ancient and modern. He made a daring escape from each one. Luckily, the guards still haven't found him.

ABOUT THE ILLUSTRATOR

Patricio Clarey was born in 1978 in Argentina. He graduated in fine arts at the School of Visual Arts Martín Malharro, specializing in illustration and graphic design. Patricio currently lives in Barcelona, Spain, where he works as a freelance graphic designer and illustrator. He has created several comics and graphic novels, and his work has been featured in several books and other publications.